A WANDER IN THE WOODS

Super Stories

Edited By Allie Jones

First published in Great Britain in 2021 by:

 Young**Writers**® Est. 1991

Young Writers
Remus House
Coltsfoot Drive
Peterborough
PE2 9BF
Telephone: 01733 890066
Website: www.youngwriters.co.uk

Printed and bound in the UK by BookPrintingUK
Website: www.bookprintinguk.com
YB0465AZ

FOREWORD

Welcome, Reader!

*Are you ready to take a Wander in the Woods?
Then come right this way - your journey to amazing
adventures awaits. It's very simple, all you have
to do is turn the page and you'll be transported
into a forest brimming with super stories.*

*Is it magic? Is it a trick? No! It's all down to the skill and
imagination of primary school pupils from around the
country. We gave them the task of writing a story and
to do it in just 100 words! I think you'll agree they've
achieved that brilliantly – this book is jam-packed with
exciting and thrilling tales, and such variety too, from
mystical portals to creepy monsters lurking in the dark!*

*These young authors have brought their ideas to life
using only their words. This is the power of creativity
and it gives us life too! Here at Young Writers we want
to pass our love of the written word onto the next
generation and what better way to do that than to
celebrate their writing by publishing it in a book!*

*It sets their work free from homework books and
notepads and puts it where it deserves to be – out in
the world and preserved forever! Each awesome author
in this book should be super proud of themselves, and
now they've got proof of their ideas and their creativity
in black and white, to look back on in years to come!*

CONTENTS

Shanaya Kotecha (10)	63
Rahul Nathwani (9)	64
Dilan Chauhan (9)	65
Divya Chauhan (10)	66
Vinaya Chavda (8)	67
Shriya Solanki (8)	68
Shivam Mistry (8)	69
Jhanvi Vyas (8)	70
Diya Kaushal (8)	71
Mahi Bhutiya (10)	72
Pavitra Patel (9)	73
Neha Bharakhada (8)	74
Keeyan Patel (8)	75
Shruti Karelia (8)	76
Arianna Parmar (8)	77
Aaryan Bapodra (9)	78
Sejal Khunti (9)	79
Elissia Dharamshi (8)	80
Mayan Mehta (9)	81
Heerav Chudasama (8)	82
Leah Mapara (9)	83
Avi Patel (8)	84
Tanish Patel (9)	85
Heer Jethwa (12)	86
Shania Desai (8)	87

St Benedict's Catholic Primary School, Hindley

Zara Hassan (11)	88
Poppy Hodgson (10)	89
Finlay Foster (10)	90
Callum Jones (11)	91
Cameron Tolley (11)	92
Lucy Scarborough (10)	93
Oliver Sleikus (10)	94
Isaac Wright (11)	95
Erin Madden (10)	96
Madison Crook (10)	97
Lizzie Clarke (9)	98
Katie Harrison (10)	99
Caitlin Cunniffe (10)	100
Laurel Carey (11)	101
Mia Greeley (11)	102

Lewis Bainbridge (10)	103
Francesca Simpson (10)	104
Bobby Gibson (10)	105
Thomas Metcalfe (11)	106
Zack Prescott (9)	107
Noah Coyle (11)	108
Ava Walsh (10)	109
Harry Addis (10)	110
Emily Davidson (10)	111
Elliot Pilkington (9)	112
Harry Kay (11)	113
Karin Olejnikova (10)	114
Robbie McLaughlin (10)	115

St Margaret's CE Primary School, Stoke Golding

Martell Williamson (8)	116
Charlie Crowfoot (7)	117
Harry Macqueen (7)	118
Archie Collis (7)	119
Harriet Marshall-Rowe (7)	120
Ellie Read (7)	121
Sophia Hurley (7)	122
Bobby Mawson-Eccles (7)	123
Daniel Lees (7)	124
Lily M (7)	125
Grayson Willis (8)	126
Roy Gosling (7)	127
Imogen Fryer (7)	128
Marli Coleman (8)	129
Isobella Robinson (8)	130
Ashlyn Sharrod (7)	131
Layla Mbah (8)	132
Zachariah Smith (8)	133
Alfie Barlow (8)	134
Corey Thorp-Wrigglesworth (7)	135
Eve Tinsley (8)	136
Emily Atakli (8)	137
Tobias Wakeling (8)	138
Lily Collis (7)	139
Bensan Elijah Karra (7)	140
Erin Iliffe (7)	141
Charlie Brocklehurst (7)	142

THE
STORIES

Escape In The Woods

As the hunters stumbled past trees, they came across a haunted house. In they went! There was blood on the walls, ripped furniture, cobwebs and cracked windows.

"Grr!"

Everyone jumped.

"Arrrooo!"

Worry crashed over the gang. In hunting formation, they entered the room to find... a group of monsters! Historical, mythical, every type. Out they all dashed, but not alone though! Down the stairs, out the door, bats screeching, owls hooting and mice squeaking. Lightning and thunder plus the pouring rain. They looked back to see two of the hunters gone...

Crunch, crunch!

Thud, thud, thud...

Someone was coming...

Otis Bradbury (9)
Copley Primary School, Copley

A Ghostly Encounter

I gently push the creaky gates to my favourite abandoned woods, but I'm stopped in my tracks when I see a beautiful pale ring. I slowly bend down to grab the ring and I gently slide it onto my finger. *Poof!* Suddenly, these white figures appear. "Have you heard about Linda?" is buzzing all around me.

I sadly remember my departed friend Linda.

"Apparently she's rotting!"

Rotting?

"W-who is? Linda," I whisper.

The ghosts stand, well hover, in shock.

"Follow us child."

I rush after them and there she is hanging from a tree, ghostly white...

Mollie Howarth (10)

Copley Primary School, Copley

The Witch, The Gloomy Forest And I

It was a terrifying, freezing night. The mist engulfed me, branches towered over me, the only light was the torch I held. I heard scuttling in the leaves surrounding me. I shivered as owls twittered faintly. I whispered comfortingly, "The witch isn't here." Although I knew she would be. My torch flickered and suddenly shattered. I lost my sight which guided me safely through the petrifying, intimidating forest. I slumped on the ground, devastated, when a shadow loomed over me, cackling. I was carelessly lifted by the arms and dumped painfully on the hard floor under a blistering green substance...

Aidan Coulthard (10)
Copley Primary School, Copley

The Mysterious Figure!

On a cold night, a boy called John was walking in the woods. There was a rustling behind John. "Hello?" exclaimed John. "Anyone there?" The rustling was getting closer and closer. John started to run. He checked if the mysterious figure was running after him and the figure was behind him so John carried on. He tried to find his way home, but he was lost. "Oh no!" shouted John. "I'm stuck out here with no shelter!"

"I will get you!" said the mysterious figure.

John carried on running, he got to the edge of a cliff and fell...

Archie (9)
Copley Primary School, Copley

The Girl In The Long-Lost Door

A thousand centuries ago I was looking for my long-lost dog in the dull, dark woods. I heard rustling in the trees and bats whistling. I got curious so I followed the whistling. I found a gold, dusty door, I stepped into a mysterious world. It trapped me! I shouted, "Help!" but no answer. "Is anyone there?" I said, but still no answer.

I found a footprint so I followed it, it led me to a haunted town. I heard a rocking chair, it was getting closer.

"Anyone?" I repeated. My voice echoed away. "Arrgh!"

Isobel Brooks (9)

Copley Primary School, Copley

Don't Go Camping At Midnight

On a dark stormy night, there was a boy called John, he was camping with his best friend Luke. Suddenly, the fire went out, they were petrified! Then they heard rustling in the bushes. They went to have a closer look but nothing was there. Then a tree fell down. They looked at the tree but nothing was there again. Then Luke said, "It's midnight." Then they heard howling in the distance. They went exploring around the forest, but there was nothing there. Then the howling returned, the leaves rustled and a monster came out and ate them!

Evan Matthews (10)
Copley Primary School, Copley

The Haunted House

One day, a group of kids wandered into the haunted woods. As they walked through the woods, they saw a mysterious mansion. Suddenly, a thunderstorm began, they took shelter in the house. They opened the door and walked in. The door closed behind them. They explored the mansion and found weapons and one found a secret passageway. He slid down it and it opened up to a dark room with a cauldron, broomstick and a black cat.

Suddenly, a figure came shooting down the slide. The figure had a wart, a black pointy hat and was wearing a black dress...

Amos Wainwright (8)
Copley Primary School, Copley

Evil Peppa Pig!

Once upon a time, Peppa Pig went to the woods for a family trip. She was collecting wood for a fire. Then she saw the most delicious-looking mushroom in the world! She picked it from the ground and swallowed it because she is a pig. Her ears turned big and her teeth turned to fangs. Finally, her eyes went red! She was returning back to camp when she heard her family laughing. Peppa didn't like that! She ran as fast as she could and shouted in her loudest voice, "I've got the logs!"
Then she gobbled them up in one!

Arthur Woodhead (9)
Copley Primary School, Copley

Ghost Woods

One day, a man called Dennis Root was driving to the windy woods for a walk. Once he arrived, he set off through the dangerous woods. As he got deeper into the woods he heard the sound of a man screaming. Dennis started walking faster. The deafening scream was enough. Then two other screams occurred, one louder than the other. Dennis started running back to his car, terrified of what he'd heard. A twig snapped behind him, but when he turned back nothing was there. When he reached his car, he was shocked to see his car was broken...

Declan O'Callaghan
Copley Primary School, Copley

The Mysterious Shadow

There was a family lurking in the woods and they thought they were being chased by someone, but then it went quiet. Later, they saw a shadow while they were toasting marshmallows, they thought it might be a killer clown because they saw a big circle nose and curly hair. Then they lost their little boy, so they went to find him. They couldn't find him but the clown was chasing them, so they thought it'd taken Timmy. Then the clown got them, but they escaped. Then they found Timmy on the floor, everyone was sad and crying.

Lexie Moses (10)
Copley Primary School, Copley

A Wander In The Woods

Gradually, the horizon became tinted pink. I walked towards the woods, I decided to have a brief meander around. I strolled deeper into the woods. I lost track of time and rapidly a fog fell around me. I no longer knew where I was and it was dark now. Skeletons of trees surrounded me like dead bones in a graveyard reaching out to take me.

"Oooh! Ha, ha, ha!"

I screamed. I had never believed ghost stories. I should have. I can't remember which ghost it was that took me, but I never saw my family again...

Elodee Walker Watene (10)

Copley Primary School, Copley

The Forest Ghost

Me and my dog are in the woods looking for my house key. I've been searching for hours, barely noticing the night growing colder and darker. A great cloud of mist is engulfing the entire forest. I go deeper in yet find nothing. Suddenly, I hear an odd wailing, almost a cry for help. I run to the strange noise, and see her, a ghost girl, sitting on a small rusty bench. There it is - the key!
I slowly approach and grab it. She turns around. I dash from the forest, down the street and I'm home. I'm safe. Until...

Jessica Myers O'Connell (10)
Copley Primary School, Copley

Flora Blossom Goes For A Wander

It was a lovely spring morning where the birds were singing beautifully. Flora Blossom was going out. She went on a walk, picking plants for tea, until... she saw the mushrooms. She tasted one mushroom and *poof!* she turned into a bunny! She heard footsteps behind her, there was a group of foxes, but they got distracted and ran away. A boy walked past but nothing happened until he heard a squeaking noise, so he bent down. He didn't know what to do to help Flora, so he took her to his house and he kept her as a pet.

Sofia Gornall (8)
Copley Primary School, Copley

The Mysterious Woods!

One winter's day a boy and his friends were trudging through the woods, it was all going well until... They came across a key! Ahead, there was a keyhole in the tree bark. They opened it and bam! Suddenly ghosts came out, flooding the woods with howls. The boys were traumatised. The howling ghosts began to chase them. It had started to go dark and they couldn't see. They ran and ran. One of them tripped over a rock and they got taken and were never seen again. The boys who made it swore they would never speak of it...

Cassius Bradbury (10)
Copley Primary School, Copley

A Trip To The Woods

Once upon a time, there was a boy called Coby. Coby and his friends Alfie, Callum and Joelan went on a walk in the woods. Before they knew it, they could not see absolutely anything because of the amount of fog. As the day went by, the fog got heavier and heavier. They started to hear ominous thudding footsteps from somewhere in the huge, terrifying, haunted woods. They ran and ran until they could run no further. Coby and his friends did not have a single clue where they could be. What could they do, it was pitch-black...?

Boden Murfin (11)
Copley Primary School, Copley

The Squirrels' Acquaintence

Once upon a time, an orphan called Chestnut went for a walk in the woods. It was morning and she met a family of squirrels. From that day on they were firm friends. Five years later, the squirrels adopted her. After the adoption ceremony, Chestnut heard a rustle in the bushes. Suddenly, wolves jumped out from everywhere! One of the squirrels gave Chestnut a diamond sword. They said, "Use it wisely." She took it, she went to each wolf and killed it. The only one left was the pup. Chestnut decided to adopt the pup.

Grace Mott (9)
Copley Primary School, Copley

The Adventure In The Woods

In the mysterious forest, a full moon appeared. Suddenly, werewolves began to howl and bats were flying all around. A man could hear owls hooting and a fog began to appear. There was an eerie figure moving, but then a twig snapped. The man discovered a haunted house and started to search. He found a room with a coffin. The coffin opened and the candles blew out. A vampire slowly came out of the coffin and the door slammed shut! The man jumped out of the window with a werewolf on his tail. He never saw daylight again...

Ava Wainwright (10)
Copley Primary School, Copley

The Story Of The Wolf Family

In a dense forest, a wolf family lived. Their names were Winston, Wanda, Wendy and Wilson. Their appetites were different to other wolves, they ate deer and rabbits.

One day, the wolf family had just had their meal and were on their way home to rest when they met up with a giant moose. Winston decided to kill the moose, but just before he could attack it, the moose roughly pushed him away. He was badly hurt but Wanda and the rest did not give up. A few minutes later, the moose was defeated and Winston was healed.

Kaiden Graham (10)
Copley Primary School, Copley

The Dead Girl!

I'm not sure, should I go in? The boy hesitates for a moment but then goes into the dark, gloomy forest, he hears light footsteps following him, he ignores it for a while but he starts to get anxious so he runs and runs. He gets deeper and deeper into the forest and hides. He hears someone running and turns around, seeing that looks like a dead girl holding a knife, coming for him. He runs again for miles and loses the dead girl. He walks in fear of the ominous child, then blacks out and never awakes...

Sophie Prag (10)
Copley Primary School, Copley

The Worst Camping Trip Ever!

At night on a camping trip with my mum and dad we were toasting marshmallows when the fire went out. My parents went in opposite directions in the woods, I was left alone. Nobody came, it was getting dark, it was almost midnight. I heard leaves rustling, I thought it was just a rat, until a clown popped out of the bush juggling knives! Bats surrounded me, the clown was getting closer, he threw his three knives at me but missed. I ran to the car and drove home as fast as possible. When home I locked all the doors!

Ollie Hunt (10)
Copley Primary School, Copley

The Lost World

One day, a boy found a plane in the woods. He called all his friends and they boarded the plane. It got attacked by pteranodons. They pulled the plane apart. The boy found a machine gun and shot everything he could, then he found a parachute! He jumped out of the plane onto the island of Sorna, The Lost World. He soon found a tree to rest in for the night.
Suddenly... crash! A tree fell down, then another and another. He then heard a roar and turned around to find two T-rexes. They bit him and ate him!

Gabriel Guy (8)
Copley Primary School, Copley

The Dark Night

I ran. Where was I? A shiver went down my throat as I felt someone or something watching me. Was I dreaming?

I ran until it hurt. I didn't know why I did, it was instinct. I stumbled but I kept going. Eventually I banged my head on a tree, but I could still feel something watching me. I just lay there, all I could see was a pile of leaves next to me. But then a hand came out and grabbed me. I screamed, "No!" but it was too late.

A lost, dark soul now wanders the woods, searching...

Henry Montesinos Walker (9)
Copley Primary School, Copley

The Haunted Camping Trip

One day, a little girl called Scarlet went on a camping trip with her family and friends. Her mum asked her to go and get some firewood, so she said yes and off she went. She found some good wood and looked up at the moon and said in her head, "What a beautiful moon."

All of a sudden, she saw a big shadow lurking behind her. She got really frightened and started to scream really loudly. She didn't dare turn around but something touched her head and took her away forever and ever.

Katie Fryer (9)
Copley Primary School, Copley

In The Dark Woods

In the dark woods there was a girl who was all alone, or so she thought. She carried on walking until she heard something, but she carried on walking deeper and deeper until she tripped up and saw bones everywhere. She felt like she was going to pass out. All of a sudden, a clown jumped out, in the blink of an eye she ran but he caught up with her and grabbed her. She got away, her heart was racing, but she carried on running until he got her again. She tried to get away, but was never seen again.

Harrison Rose (9)
Copley Primary School, Copley

The Girl At The Back Of The Bus

Five years ago there was a girl called Luna. She was on a school trip, but it went wrong. She got on the bus and off she went. Luna had to sit at the back because there was no more room. She sat next to this boy dressed in black clothes. *Who is he?* she thought.

The bus stopped for some reason. Someone was outside and the boy in black wasn't there anymore. There was a crack in the glass. It was getting late... A clown was at the door. A shadow, she ran. She was lost in the woods!

Erin Campling (9)
Copley Primary School, Copley

Lost In The Woods

Ten years ago...
It was a cold, dark night. A boy whose name was Steve decided to take a wander in the woods. People said that the woods were haunted, but Steve didn't think that. Suddenly he got lost and the only thing around him were the bones of humans and when he looked behind him he saw a dead fox. He fainted with fear.
He got back up and kept going forwards. There was a haunted house. He opened the door and saw a shadow. He ran as fast as he could, but was never seen again...

Phoebe Varley (9)
Copley Primary School, Copley

Ghost Run

As I entered the woods, the ominous mist poured through me. Before I knew it I couldn't see one bit. I kept on walking, thinking it would clear away, then all of a sudden... *crunch!* I looked around, then I saw it, it was a ghost! I sprinted for my life but I didn't know where I was. Briskly, I weaved through the trees. After three minutes of sprinting I hid behind a tree for a little break. I looked behind the titanic tree and the ghost was still following. I ran for the exit...

Aaron Edwards (10)
Copley Primary School, Copley

A Marriage Story

Once, there lived a vampire. Then another vampire came to his home. The vampire came out and they met. He proposed to her. They started planning their wedding. Then they took a wander in the woods. They got married in the woods, then 20 years later they had a walk in the same woods. They had babies and the whole family went hunting in the woods. They hunted a magic bunny that turned them back into humans. They lived in a big house but one night, in their sleep they turned into vampires again...

Rosie Emmett (8)

Copley Primary School, Copley

Rap-Unzel

Not so long ago there was a girl. She lived in a great woods in a tall tower.

One day, she said, "I want to be famous!" She was great at rapping and every time she played a sick beat her nails would grow. She texted every prince and asked them to rescue her. They all came but got freaked out by her nails. She decided to get out herself. Rap-Unzel cut her nails really sharp and safely got down. When she did she rapped at parties and she even went on world tours! She was the best!

Riya Kanetkar (10)
Copley Primary School, Copley

Wild Wolves And Me

One misty night, whilst I slept, I heard a mysterious creaking noise. Quickly I woke up, I saw white hairs. Instantly I knew it was a wolf. To the woods I travelled. When I got there I saw five wolves, each with a different shade of red eyes. At the front was a white wolf, half the size of a tree! Each stalked towards me. Concerned, I spoke softly until I noticed a brown female had a thorn in her leg. I slowly approached and pulled it out. They looked at me gratefully and then I left for good.

Sadie Normington (9)
Copley Primary School, Copley

The Wild Woods

I need some fresh air, there are some woods nearby so I go for a wander. It's a gloomy day, I step in, then *bang!* I drop down unconscious.
I wake up under a tree, the sound of hooting owls and howling wolves is close by. How long was I unconscious? I stand up, where am I? I walk across a bridge, then a path and I see a man clutching rocks. Is that the person who hit me? I walk up to them, ready to fight, but they offer to help me. Suddenly, a bear comes up behind us...

Milo Walker (8)

Copley Primary School, Copley

The Killer In The Woods

On a dull, cold and dismal day, my friends and I were playing rugby. Until... we came across a cursed woods. Of course we went to investigate. There were trees, flowers and birds singing surrounding us. Time went fast and it was hours later that we set off for home. But which way was it? As we came to a dead end, all we could see was a black figure over the wall, staring us deep in the eyes. It started to move towards us. We all ran. I tripped and fell and got dragged into the leaves...

Zach Taylor (10)
Copley Primary School, Copley

The Bear Chaser!

Once upon a time, there were four young girls who were going on a nice walk in the woods. Along the way, the girls came across a big black shadow. They thought it was a bear, but they kept on walking. Moments later a grizzly bear was creeping up on them as they were chatting happily to one another. Then suddenly a huge shadow towered over all of them! As they turned and screamed, the bear charged. In horror all four girls ran home. As they got home they heard a big knock on the door...

Mia Taylor (8)
Copley Primary School, Copley

The Woods

I was walking in the woods on my own, it was extremely dark and I had no idea what the time was, my phone was dead. Whatever could I do? I was walking and something tapped me. I realised nothing was behind me though. There was only one thing it could be - ghost!

I ran and ran through the woods and I saw a gate. I tried to get out but something grabbed me and held me back. I eventually got out then I sprinted back home. I got there and couldn't tell my mum. What an experience!

Declan O'Dowd (10)

Copley Primary School, Copley

The Ghost Driver

Me and my friends were playing in the woods and, all of a sudden, we heard footsteps and the crunching of leaves. It was just a fox. We heard a car in the distance. Suddenly we heard a bang in the darkness. Twenty minutes later we went and checked it out. The car was in a ditch so we slid down and there was a body on the floor covered in blood. I touched it, it was soft, but it jumped up and chased us deeper into the woods! We hid behind a tree, we thought we were safe, until...

Rueben Higginson (11)
Copley Primary School, Copley

The Mysterious Woods

One night, in the mysterious, dark and deadly woods, noise rattled in a bush. I couldn't see anything, all I found was an item. All I could ask myself was, what is this? As I walked towards the bush, I saw something. Was it a ghost? It was! I turned and ran. Wait, maybe the item I found could help? Then I found a campfire as ominous clouds covered my head. The ghost came back. Off I ran again and got the item out of my backpack, hoping it would help. The ghost followed...

Jessica Gornall (10)
Copley Primary School, Copley

The Dark Figure!

Deep in the dense and dark woods, there were lots of eyes watching me, as well as crows. I checked over my shoulder, to see a dark shadow with huge hands stalking me. Then I took another glance and he was right behind me. He grabbed me and took me to his cellar and trapped me there. Just when I thought I was going to die, everything got worse - rats, mice and spiders! To my surprise, a huge pack of wolves came to rescue me and ate all the mice, rats and spiders in a rampage.

Sonni Gledhill (9)
Copley Primary School, Copley

Wolves In The Woods

One cold night I was sleeping in a tent. Suddenly, I woke up and found my family was gone! I panicked then I went to look for them. As I was looking I heard a far-off howl, it got closer and closer. I was being chased by wolves! I kept running but they got closer with every step. The next thing I heard was eight shots of a gun. I saw a mysterious man in the shadows with the gun. I went up to him to say thank you for saving me but he disappeared and everything went silent.

Elsa Sandford
Copley Primary School, Copley

Vampire Mansion

On a cold, dark night, a girl called Rose left her house for a walk. Even though there were vampires on the loose, she ran to the woods. She had been out for an hour and spotted a gloomy house. Rose ran to the strange house and knocked on the vast wooden door. It seemed really thick so she didn't know if she was heard. She stepped forward and there were two people staring at her. They ran forward and she screamed. Rose, the 13-year-old girl, was never seen again.

Robyn Hare (10)
Copley Primary School, Copley

What A Day!

Today was a good day, I got a lot of treats and pats! To start the day me and my owner went to the woods. I met some dogs! Then we walked back home, to find the door locked. Who was it? Were they eating my food? The door creaked open when I pushed it. I heard a bang. I ran to the garden and saw a vicious, wild bear! Its sharp teeth grinned at me, but I walked outside as brave as I could ever be! Was this the last time I would see the bear again?

Annabelle Mulley-Quinn (9)
Copley Primary School, Copley

The Haunted Forest

Once there was a forest, but not just an ordinary forest, at night it became haunted and in the day it was enchanted. In the day there were rainbow unicorns and beautiful nature, but at night it became dark and rainy, there were evil unicorns and scary ghosts.

One night, a little girl and her dad came, the little girl was walking and she saw an evil unicorn, so she ran to tell her dad, but her dad was dead. A wolf had killed him...

Polly Szefer (9)
Copley Primary School, Copley

In The Woods!

Once, there was a girl in the woods and she was running away from a grizzly bear! Luckily, there was a go-kart race, so she jumped on the back of one. But the go-kart flipped up and she got stuck in a tree. She couldn't get down. There was a bin lid on the floor, so she crashed to the floor and slid on the lid down a hill and landed in a boat. It was moving and rowing but there was no one on it! It was a mystery, was it a ghost?

Angel Palmer (8)
Copley Primary School, Copley

Lost In The Woods

Once upon a time, there was a little boy called Tom. He lived in the woods.

One day, as he was happily walking in the woods, he got lost... As the huge trees loomed over him he heard scary noises screeching. As the ground and trees got darker, he heard a black bear. So he climbed up a tree and got his slingshot out...

Freddie George Garthwaite (9)
Copley Primary School, Copley

A World Under A Rainbow

"I wish I could meet an elf," sighed Hamza longingly.

Mariam noticed their grandmother's mirror starting to glow. She nudged Hamza towards it. The children found themselves lying flat on their backs staring at an immense rainbow. All around them, fluttering fairies and excited elves went about their business. Suddenly, a peculiar-looking pixie blew softly on her horn. As if by magic, a grand table appeared filled with delicious treats. Carried by hundreds of fairies, the guests were invited to join the feast. After much laughter, music and scrumptious food, it was time for the children to go home.

Mariam Soliman (9)

Hamilton Academy, High Wycombe

Sally's Adventure

Sally was on her school field trip, it was a camping trip. She was on the bus, wondering what would happen. She got there, her class were singing songs, then it was bedtime. There was a door in one of the trees, she went through it.
"Woah!" Sally was in a beautiful land of flowers. Sally was amazed, she heard music, it was coming from a flower. She touched the flower. A butterfly appeared, it looked like a fairy. Sally said, "Can you help me?"
The butterfly said, "Yes," then she said, "bye-bye," and Sally was back in her tent.

Tahiyatt Zain (8)
Hamilton Academy, High Wycombe

Cyber The Robot Horse

There was once a girl called Felix. One day, her mum and dad went out for some shopping. She had been hoping she would be able to explore the forbidden room. She opened the door and fell into a teleporter. She finally landed in a circuit world and met a robo-horse called Cyber.

"Who are you?" said Cyber.

"I'm a girl," called Felix.

"Come to my battery house," said Cyber.

At his house, Felix sat by the electric fire and fed Cyber some halo grass as she gently fell asleep. Cyber then let Felix go to her bed.

Aadya Jena (8)
Hamilton Academy, High Wycombe

An Orange Door!

There was a young girl called Shalina Welllington. Her long hair twisted around making an incredibly tangled mess on top of her head. She lived with her old grandmother in the Nowhere Woods, the trees would whisper and talk amongst themselves (like chatting old ladies).

Shalina absolutely loved new adventures. She went looking around the small cottage to find something exciting - she did. An orange door. She had never seen this before, so carefully opened it and stepped in. To her surprise there in front of her eyes stood her missing parents...

Jessie-Rose Jaques (9)
Hamilton Academy, High Wycombe

Bella

Once upon a time, there lived a girl called Bella. One day, while she was exploring her attic, Bella found a dusty, old, shimmery box with something glowing inside. As she lifted the lid she found a glistening necklace.

Curiously, she put it on and was suddenly transported into a far away, frozen land. She found a cave and rested for the night.

The next morning, Bella jumped up and ran through the forest trying to find her way home. She took off the necklace and put it back on. It started to glow again and Bella magically returned home.

Khadija Ahmed (9)
Hamilton Academy, High Wycombe

The Cursed Cupboard

It was a calm, breezy spring day. Lea and Leo were playing hide-and-seek. It was Lea's turn to count. Leo scanned the room from left to right, *the cupboard*, he thought. Little did he know the cupboard was cursed. It was a portal to the dimension of the dead. Leo dashed to the cupboard and hid. He scrunched up into a ball and made as least noise as possible.

"Three, two, one... ready or not, here I come." Lea searched everywhere. She was nearing the cupboard where Leo was being sucked into the dimension of the dead...

Halimah Manzoor (8)
Hamilton Academy, High Wycombe

Kira's Nightmare

There was a girl called Kira. One day she was going to school, instead of walking Kira took the bus. The bus suddenly stopped next to a mysterious gate. Kira jumped out of the bus and slowly walked to the gate and opened it. As she walked through the gate woods appeared. She could see trees so tall she couldn't see the top. There was purple mist and scary shadows everywhere shaped like monsters! She heard spooky noises so she turned around and ran back. She tripped and banged her head. Kira woke up and realised it was a nightmare.

Andrea Morar (9)
Hamilton Academy, High Wycombe

The Magic Book

On a rainy day, when Skylair finished reading her book, she decided to choose another book. Surprisingly, she found a book she'd never seen. She opened it and started to read. She went to get a chair. Suddenly, she tripped on a toy and fell in the book. Skylair landed in some water, in front of her was a mermaid named Ashley. She told Skylair that she had to collect two items, the first one was in the enchanted forest behind a hideous cave, the second was in a shell. A portal appeared and she went through it back home.

Emaan Tariq (8)
Hamilton Academy, High Wycombe

The Gem

There was a little boy called Paul, he always loved going to his grandma's house because she had all kinds of gems. Paul loved the half-red and half-gold gem, but was never allowed to touch it. This morning he went to his grandma's house and sneaked to the attic, he found and took the gem, but then he got sucked in and got trapped in a castle. He knew how to whistle and how to do a dragon call and that's what he did. A big slimy dragon came that smelt like swamp or garbage, but it saved Paul.

Prajwal Mallya (8)
Hamilton Academy, High Wycombe

The Mirror

Once upon a time, a girl called Lily went on holiday with her parents. Her room was big and she had a big mirror. After Lily had dinner with her parents they fell asleep, so then Lily got bored so she went to the mirror that she'd glimpsed earlier, then she got sucked in! It was dark and scary, but suddenly she saw something - it was a dragon! It came closer and invited Lily for tea. She went with him but she forgot she had to go home. She ran as fast as she could back to her parents.

Samah Azad (8)
Hamilton Academy, High Wycombe

Dragon Trainers

There was once a little boy called George, he was in nursery. George looked out of the window and saw a sad dragon. George ran outside. George tried to touch the dragon but it wouldn't let him touch it. George got food for the dragon and it ate it in one bite. The dragon became friends with George, then it heard people crying. The dragon saved them and lots of dragons, then the dragon grew and grew and then it was time to let the dragon go. They said goodbye and it left.

Humzah Barekzai (12)
Hamilton Academy, High Wycombe

The Mirror

One day, there was a boy. In his old cottage there was a sparkly mirror. He tried to touch the twisty corner, but each time it shocked his finger. Then suddenly a portal showed up, he went in and landed in a wood. He felt ill when all the trees started toppling down on him. He saw a dragon and he touched it and the dragon opened his fiery eyes. Luckily he was a friendly dragon and he took him back to the portal, he hopped off and went back through.

Ismael Malik
Hamilton Academy, High Wycombe

The Woods

Masses of trees dominated him. Necromancy had dominated the forest with an aura of vulnerability. It was twilight and an angelical choir could be heard descending from the sky. The woods were growing darker, the boy stopped and sat down, leaning against a tree. Multicoloured mushrooms grew to his left and above him the trees were bearing little leaves. He hesitated before closing his eyes and within seconds he fell asleep.
A resonance awoke the boy. "Who's there?" he whispered. He observed furtively. In his chest, he had the feeling of impending danger. Someone or something suddenly replied, "I'm here..."

Alisha Mistry (10)
Krishna Avanti Primary School, Evington

The Dragon's Feast!

A witch heard footsteps. "I'm a dragon as mean as can be, I'm planning to have you with my chips for tea!"

The witch thought quick and replied, "Well, if you're so hungry I'll give you something tastier..."

"Children I want!" replied the dragon.

The witch stumbled upon two lost children and cast a spell on them to lure them. "Lovely children, are you lost? I can help but first pick some blueberries!"

Unknowingly, the blueberries were poisonous and the hungry children ate them and froze. The dragon saw them and gobbled them in a flash but the dragon lied...

Esha Modha (8)

Krishna Avanti Primary School, Evington

The Mysterious Forest

It was time to go. Elizabeth packed her bag and was ready. *Beep! Beep!* The bus was waiting for her. She clambered down the stairs and got on the bus. The journey was exhausting but they were finally at Mongrave Forest. Suddenly, *whoosh, whoosh*, two people were missing but nobody realised. They got their heavy camping tents and set them up.

Whoosh! Whoosh! Everyone else was gone! Elizabeth was alone.

Crack!

"Argh!" She fell into a hole. The world was like it flipped over, like a turtle on its back. This world had rainbow dinosaurs flying and peacocks...

Zoya Chatterjee (11)
Krishna Avanti Primary School, Evington

An Evening In The Woods

Everybody had been talking about the mysterious house in the woods. As the scientist walked through the enchanted, overgrown woods, he saw different types of insects, trees then finally saw the mysterious house. The house was dark and looked haunted and scary. He took a deep breath and walked inside, gripping his torch tightly. Spooky witches and vampires with glowing green teeth appeared and his heart started beating like a brass drum. The scientist ran as fast as a cheetah even though he had not finished his frightening adventure. He said, "I am never going back to the haunted house again!"

Anay Mistry (9)
Krishna Avanti Primary School, Evington

The Hidden World!

"Oh no, why did you kick the ball into the woods?" shouted John at Sam.

They ran into the woods, hoping to find the ball. As they ran, they both slipped and tumbled into a scary and secret passage! To their surprise, two ghost knights were staring at them. "Hello," said Sam, terrified.

"Ah, sorry, my name is Sir Knight and this is Sir Blackban," one knight said shyly.

"We want to go home," said Sam.

"Okay, follow the track and it will take you to the end."

Like magic, they found their home and their mum made them pie.

Nandakishore Mundalappa (8)

Krishna Avanti Primary School, Evington

Wacky And Jacky's Imaginary World

Wacky and Jacky are best friends. One hot day they went into the woods to play. As they played, they came across a mysterious but uncanny-looking tree. Approaching this tree, a powerful source sucked them in. Both fell to the bottom with a thud. Upon waking, they found themselves in an extraordinary world. They looked around and were dumbfounded with what they saw - people walking upside down, food flying like UFOs and people talking gibberish. It was just like Alice's Wonderland. Amazed by the weird atmosphere, they indulged in flying treats. The rest can be left up to your imagination!

Yogiraj Dixit (9)

Krishna Avanti Primary School, Evington

Camping Trip In The Woods

A group of friends were having a meeting at Thomas's treehouse, they decided to go camping. They set off for a camping site with their belongings and rucksacks. They arrived at the woods, which looked scary, creepy, gloomy and cold. The group were exhausted from travelling as Thomas led the way with a compass, walking along rocky stinging nettles across the path. The group arrived in the woodlands with bare trees surrounding them. They started setting up camp in the clearing. James went off to find wood for the campfire and the rest worried because it was late...

Nihal Jitesh Patel (8)
Krishna Avanti Primary School, Evington

Where Am I?

Once upon a time, there were two twins called Mary and Bill. They were in their bedroom, until something caught Mary's eye. It was big and tall and was a door. They opened it and found themselves underground. "Where are we?" Bill's voice echoed. Bill had seen a light. The two twins rapidly ran. *Whoosh!* They found themselves in the woods. They went for a wander in the woods. There was a castle.

"Let's go in!"

They opened the door. *Whoosh!* They were back in their bedroom, lying on their beds. What a dream!

Shanaya Kotecha (10)
Krishna Avanti Primary School, Evington

The Forest Guardian

Once upon a time, there was a ferocious black, gold and blue dragon named... 'The Terror Tooth'! This mighty beast guarded the frightening forest. But what the dragon didn't know was, that there was a little wooden cottage nearby, and in that cottage there was a father called Boris and a nine-year-old boy called Ray.

One dark, foggy morning, Ray's father was still sleeping, so Ray decided to go out into the forest. Suddenly, Ray saw a red light in the sky, it was the dragon! He landed with a thump! Ray went to investigate... then got eaten!

Rahul Nathwani (9)
Krishna Avanti Primary School, Evington

The Identical Forest

In a world like no other, Jez was playing happily when he slipped and his hand hit a stone covered in moss...

"Do not touch or there will be consequences!"

Swoosh! Suddenly, Jez twirled like a tornado into a forest identical to the one he was in but now it was pitch-black! In the blink of an eye, blinding fire was heading straight towards him. Petrified, the fire crackled and made Jez shiver. A circle of fire suddenly surrounded the boy, while all the bushes were burning into smithereens. "Argh!" Jez was never seen again.

Dilan Chauhan (9)

Krishna Avanti Primary School, Evington

Wishful Woods

Embraced by tall trees, Amber and her family were strolling to the top of the hill at Wishful Woods. Blackberry bushes and stinging nettles stood amongst them while wild hedges loomed over listening to their secrets. Amber sat on the ancient stone sundial when suddenly... *poof!* She was gone! Moments later, Amber landed on the rock-hard ground with a thud. Shaking in fear, Amber crept through the darkness into the beaming light. Suddenly, all eyes lay on her. To her surprise, the beasts smiled and the fairies roared. What was she meant to do now...?

Divya Chauhan (10)
Krishna Avanti Primary School, Evington

Magic Fairies

One day in the woods, Lily and Eve, the fairies, were having a great time. Lily was admiring the woods and Eve was collecting flowers, they were laughing until they heard something. It was a siren. A robber was taking money from the bank! Immediately, the robber went left, the fairies followed without knowing the police were looking in the woods for the criminal. The girls found the police and told them the direction. After a few minutes of walking they found the criminal. The police sent him to jail and the fairies could finally have peace again.

Vinaya Chavda (8)
Krishna Avanti Primary School, Evington

The 'Deadly' Prank

Five friends bought a lovely mansion in Buckingham. They planned a games night. That was when the floorboards started creaking and strange episodes began happening. They didn't think much of it at first, then on the 31st January 2024, Lucy found a body in the loft. It was a beautiful blonde girl, about thirteen years old. The girls rushed and called the police. The wind blew strong and the tree branches danced. It felt like it was the day, the deadly day. The police finally caught the killer. It was their friend Mellisa but it was all a prank!

Shriya Solanki (8)
Krishna Avanti Primary School, Evington

Wolfy Grandma

It was a dark, cold evening and Red Riding Hood was making her way to Grandma's house on the other side of the dark woods. As she entered the woods, she could see tall trees with overhanging branches that looked like huge hands about to grab her. The wind was whistling through the trees and the sound of a wolf howling could be heard, which scared Red Riding Hood. This made her walk faster with her heart pounding.

When she reached Grandma's house the front door was wide open and she went upstairs to see a wolf turning into Grandma...

Shivam Mistry (8)

Krishna Avanti Primary School, Evington

The Mysterious Path

Dear Diary,

It was getting dark, Stacey and I were told to collect some wood for the fire. We were sent in twos. Halfway, during our search, we came across two trees shaped like an arch, creating a path for us to enter. The air became crisp, shivers ran down our spines. Was something wrong? Our curiosity was taking over us. With no hesitation, we sauntered through without looking back. The wind wailed, warning us not to go through. The trees swayed, trying to block us before we took another step. That was when we knew something was wrong...

Jhanvi Vyas (8)
Krishna Avanti Primary School, Evington

The Ghosts!

On a sunny day, there was a family of ghosts! They lived on a large hill behind lots of prickly green bushes.

A family of humans were on a hike nearby.

"Mum, can we climb that hill?" asked a small girl.

"Sure sweetie," said the mum.

Now the humans were climbing near the ghosts' house! The ghosts frighteningly flew up behind them and chased them into the darkness of the house. They slammed the door shut behind them. The mum screamed for help, but it was too late. What was to become of them...?

Diya Kaushal (8)

Krishna Avanti Primary School, Evington

The Door

One inky, thrilling night, a group of intelligent kids were excited about the candy they were going to get. Mia, Miya, Jordan and Jayden, suddenly saw an extraordinary tree with a door on it. They were curious. Mia, with a lack of courage stepped up and opened the awkward door. Before them, was a gorgeous park that made the children's mouths open. Without a word, they stepped in the door, in the blink of an eye the door disappeared! *Whoosh!* One hundred metres away was another door, so they sprinted and they were back home.

Mahi Bhutiya (10)

Krishna Avanti Primary School, Evington

A Camping Trip

Once upon a time, there was a boy called Jack and his sister Bella. They went camping in the large woods, they were wandering in the terrifying woods which was filled with creepy-crawlies. It was a really dark night, however they continued walking in the woods. Bella jumped because she noticed a snake hiss. "Hiss!" Suddenly, they noticed something flying in the sky. It was a chariot led by horses. They sat on it and it started going towards their house. They reached their house safely where their mother was waiting for them.

Pavitra Patel (9)

Krishna Avanti Primary School, Evington

Lost In The Woods

One peculiar night, everything was wrong. Sat there was a girl called Celia, she was feeling curious about what was unravelling outside so she tiptoed out. Just then, upon her was the woods. Celia went in, walking a bit. Celia looked up and she was lost. What had happened? She heard a noise creeping upon her, it was a dragon! She then saw someone, it was another girl. They became friends and found a way to beat the mysterious dragon. The ferocious animal was killed. They both went home and her parents were shocked when she told them.

Neha Bharakhada (8)

Krishna Avanti Primary School, Evington

Fire!

It was a dry evening and Kush, Keeyan, Jack and Marrie went to the forest so they could camp. When they arrived they set up a giant tent for all of the family. Soon, they found themselves in the pitch-black. Jack spoke, "Time to light the fire and tell spooky stories while eating some jam sandwiches."

"Okay Dad, can we go to sleep?" yawned Kush.

"Fine, let's go to sleep."

The boys went outside, the fire was burning! They got buckets and went to the stream and put the fire out.

Keeyan Patel (8)

Krishna Avanti Primary School, Evington

The Magic Rainbow Path

One night, an adventurous young girl had a dream that at the bottom of her garden, behind a closed green door, there was a magical path leading to a castle where the one and only dancing unicorn lived. She woke up in curiosity. Nobody ever went beyond the green door. She ran into the garden and saw a shining light from under the door. So she started walking towards the door, wondering what it could be? As she opened the door you won't believe what she saw. There it was, the magical rainbow path that led her to her dream!

Shruti Karelia (8)
Krishna Avanti Primary School, Evington

Big Bad Wolf

If you go into the woods tonight, you'll be in for a big surprise. For there is something hiding and it is called The Big Bad Wolf, The Big Bad Wolf, The Big Bad Wolf, *Roooooar!* It may be here, it may be there, for he is lurking everywhere. Tiptoe, tiptoe, for he knows where you'll go. Tiptoe, tiptoe, he hates your favourite show! He likes naughty people and his favourite treat is pickle! Do not go out after dinner, for he likes eating lots of sinners! He is as scary as a ghost - so Beware! Beware! BEWARE!

Arianna Parmar (8)
Krishna Avanti Primary School, Evington

The Unknown Reflection

On the night of the full moon, lightning and thunder hit the ground as the people stayed in their homes, however, not Jack! He was the only one who dared to step out of his house. As he walked through the streets he felt something mysterious pass his arm. It left a glimpse of light which led Jack to the only place where no one dared to step... the Cryptic Forest! Jack continued following the bright light which slowly faded away. Jack returned home and went to open the door where his reflection was an unknown shadow...

Aaryan Bapodra (9)
Krishna Avanti Primary School, Evington

Horrible Gang!

A light went on, off, on, off, so a boy called Tim went to the garden. Tim saw a black door, he opened it, there were some sparkles coming from a wand. It was a nasty witch, she had a black dress. Then there was a noise, *bang! Crash!* Then from the sea that was a lime colour was a mermaid with green hair and a shimmery, glittery tail. Tim got frightened and started to shiver. The mermaid and witch were ready to do their magic but from a tree came a ghost.

"Bye Tim."

He was back home.

Sejal Khunti (9)

Krishna Avanti Primary School, Evington

The Haunted House

One dark, stormy day, there was a broken haunted house with six rooms. All the windows were smashed and glass surrounded the windows. The glass was so sharp - the girl who entered stepped backwards. She ran to the living room and the couch started to talk. She screamed. "Argh! What are you?" she asked.

All of a sudden, the house started to talk and it became louder and louder. She said, "If you stop talking, I will do a challenge."

Her challenge was to clean the rubbish house!

Elissia Dharamshi (8)

Krishna Avanti Primary School, Evington

Matt's Adventure

One brisk day, Matt went to the woods. On entry, he saw many creatures, when he got deep into the woods he eyed a monster. The monster was tall, skinny and ugly. Matt screamed, "Argh!" as he was terrified. He fumbled and ran helter-skelter to hide. The monster was trying to catch up, but it lost track of Matt. Matt eventually found a den and hid inside it. With his bad luck, he found snakes hiding in there! He got frightened and ran as fast as he could, till he found a way out and got home.

Mayan Mehta (9)
Krishna Avanti Primary School, Evington

A Hidden World

One day, a little boy found a hidden door in his garden, it shone brighter than the sun. He stepped in and arrived at a beautiful forest with lanterns shining above him. He stepped into a boat that floated on top of a smooth glistening river. It took him to a giant golden palace. He suddenly saw a king trying to trap a beautiful blue bird. He jumped onto the flying chariot next to him and flew up to the king. He grabbed the bird and ran away, taking it to his house, to his surprise the bird stayed!

Heerav Chudasama (8)
Krishna Avanti Primary School, Evington

Looking Through The Window

Amy was going to move house and all she thought about was her new room. When she arrived, she ran upstairs. As it had been a long journey, she went to bed after dinner. Soon after, there was a nice cool breeze blowing in her face. As Amy opened her eyes, she saw a creepy clown outside her bedroom. All of a sudden, it vanished. Amy heard the front door open and hid under her covers. Her door started to creak open. The creepy clown reached for her... She opened her eyes and there was nothing there...

Leah Mapara (9)
Krishna Avanti Primary School, Evington

Camping Trip

We were getting on the minibus and were going camping in the woods. All of us were being very quiet on the minibus and we were very bored. Finally, we arrived at the woods and put up our tents. We then realised there was no Internet and we were very sad. We then started to play tag but it was too much fun and, before we knew it, it was time to cook our favourite food and go to bed. The next day, we went back home on the minibus and were chattering about how much fun we had.

Avi Patel (8)

Krishna Avanti Primary School, Evington

Mr Strong

There was once a man who was very strong. He helped many people in many different ways and was known for his good deeds.

One day, Mr Strong was walking and found Mr and Mrs Baker.

"Mr Strong, please help our children!" panicked Mrs Baker.

So Mr Strong saved them.

"Thank you Mr Strong for your help, we appreciate it very much."

"My pleasure, just call me if you need me."

Then Mr Strong walked home and went to bed.

Tanish Patel (9)

Krishna Avanti Primary School, Evington

The Magic World!

Once upon a time, lived a boy called Mike. One Sunday afternoon he was bored and wanted to play so he went to his younger sister but she was busy. Mum and Dad were cooking, so Mike went to his book corner and picked a book. Suddenly, the bookshelf split, leading to a passageway, so he went through. He saw a castle, he tried to go in but he was stopped, so he went to a waterfall. As he looked in Mike fell in, then he saw a door and went through it...

Heer Jethwa (12)
Krishna Avanti Primary School, Evington

The Magical Forest

In a faraway land, there was a doorway to the magic woods. Through the door, there was a huge tree with woodland animals big and small all around it. The great tree started to fall because of a storm, which caused a lot of damage to the woods. Unfortunately, the animals couldn't fix the tree so it fell. Without the tree the woods would be destroyed. A few minutes later the animals all worked together and fixed the problem.

Shania Desai (8)
Krishna Avanti Primary School, Evington

Freddy's Funtime Circus

Yesterday, a petrifying adventure took place. Me, Caitlin, Ava and Frankie went for a stroll in the woods, when Frankie spotted some footsteps in the mud. We followed these peculiar, alien-like muddy footprints, leading to a bare house that had queer-shaped windows. Frankie and I immediately ran inside the bizarre place without a second thought. Caitlin and Ava tagged along. Sat inside was a clown. We ran and yes, the clown chased. It was like a game of cat and mouse. Suddenly, Caitlin dashed into a mirror and disappeared!

"Turn around children."

Unfortunately we turned around...

Zara Hassan (11)

St Benedict's Catholic Primary School, Hindley

Mental

There once was a girl who lived near some woods. She loved to wander in there. One day something was different. On her daily wander, she noticed something suspicious. It was a dark figure lurking behind a tree. Without thinking, she went towards it. She knew the woods very well - nothing could hurt her in there. As she got closer, she began to hear screams and howls. At this point she realised the dark figure was in fact a woman wearing hospital gowns. The troubled woman suddenly realised she had company. She let out another scream. Things were becoming disturbing...

Poppy Hodgson (10)
St Benedict's Catholic Primary School, Hindley

The Bomb

One sunny day, three adventurous teenagers went on a walk in the woods. They were laughing and joking until suddenly the ground seemed to move from beneath their feet and they fell down into what seemed like a hidden ditch. *Crash!* Their shocked bodies hit the floor with a thud. The teenagers quickly stood up and brushed off the dirt. They glanced around. Something stood out. It was a huge black box with four wires attached to it. One of the boys picked it up without thinking. He suddenly spotted a timer on the back. It was too late. *Boom!*

Finlay Foster (10)

St Benedict's Catholic Primary School, Hindley

The Adventure In The Hidden World

One day, me, my friends and my class went to a hidden world, it was completely different to Earth (our home). It was beyond your wildest dreams, in this magical world we could see fire-breathing dragons, magical pink unicorns and horrendously horrid griffins. We also found things that blew our mind, chocolate sauce rivers, candy cane trees, strawberries dipped in chocolate and gingerbread houses.

Eventually this adventure had to end, and it did. We were very sad but it was truly amazing. We would never forget this experience, then we went home.

Callum Jones (11)
St Benedict's Catholic Primary School, Hindley

The Mad Camping School Trip

The Year 6 class went on a camping trip into the woods in the middle of the day. They were all having fun playing games, but it was soon really dark. Then they heard weird noises so they looked out and there were monsters outside the cabin! Then everyone was really scared and people were screaming like crazy. But then everything changed and the weird scary monsters somehow teleported to another world which meant they could get somewhere safe. They managed to get back to school without getting injured. They didn't think they'd go there again!

Cameron Tolley (11)
St Benedict's Catholic Primary School, Hindley

The Creature

There's a woods where nobody goes. Four friends went camping there. The day was going fine until night. They were telling ghost stories by the fire, one was about small creatures with bulging red eyes.

In the morning, when they woke up they saw something staring at them. Then they packed up immediately.

When they went back to school they told their story. The week after, other children went to look but they couldn't see anything, so the boys thought it was clear to go back, but they were wrong...

They were never seen again.

Lucy Scarborough (10)

St Benedict's Catholic Primary School, Hindley

The Demon

A boy invited his friends to go camping and tell ghost stories. When they were telling stories the campfire ran out and then came back again. His friends then disappeared, confused, he turned around, seeing his fate... A demon. The boy ran as fast as he could past the river and the campsites. He hid in one of the cabins and he remembered there was a phone in the ranger station. He ran over to it and called the police. The demon got closer... The sirens got closer...
The police arrived and searched, all that remained was the boy's hat...

Oliver Sleikus (10)
St Benedict's Catholic Primary School, Hindley

The Snowglobe!

In a normal house on a normal street, lived a boy called Alfie. One day, he took a stroll in the neighbouring woods. He couldn't believe his eyes when he came across a snowglobe... Alfie picked up the snowglobe and shook it. Suddenly, he got teleported to the North Pole! But something seemed strange... Elves were acting weirdly and Alfie saw Santa in the corner of his eye. Alfie went over to Santa and asked what was the matter. He said his evil brother had hypnotised the elves with his magic jewel. So Alfie and Santa destroyed the jewel.

Isaac Wright (11)
St Benedict's Catholic Primary School, Hindley

Don't Go Into The Woods Today

I was wandering in the woods with Daisy one night when suddenly we spotted in the corner of our eyes a mysterious bundle of leaves in a giant heap. We moved the leaves. There it was: a dead body out in the open. The next day was school and me and Daisy hadn't spoken a word about what we had seen. We wanted to erase it forever. "Can Holly and Daisy report to my office immediately?" instructed the headteacher over the speaker. We went straight there. We walked in. *Snap!* "You have nowhere to run now ladies!"

Erin Madden (10)

St Benedict's Catholic Primary School, Hindley

Cutie

Every night two girls that were roommates heard a knock at the door around 2am. They knew it was a little girl who they called Cutie. She loved to play, but one night the girls were really tired so they told Cutie they couldn't play so Cutie ran away angry. The next morning the girls told the guard about Cutie. At first he was confused but then he stopped for a moment because he realised Cutie died five years ago! He told the girls and they were scared they had been playing with a ghost...
The girls are still traumatised.

Madison Crook (10)
St Benedict's Catholic Primary School, Hindley

The Secret Book

On a Friday afternoon, walking home from school I decided to take a stroll through the woods. I started walking then I realised it was quite long so I should head back. Suddenly, the entrance disappeared, but I kept walking forwards. To my astonishment icy blue lights flickered from a tall oak tree. A hole appeared in the trunk, willing me to look inside. I put my hand in the deep, dark hole and pulled out a raggedy, rough book. It said something about leaving at 6pm and creatures. I desperately looked at my watch and to my horror...

Lizzie Clarke (9)
St Benedict's Catholic Primary School, Hindley

The Shadow...

One Wednesday, there was a Halloween party and Minny was dancing until she zoned out. She walked out to the nearby park and sat on the swing. A few minutes later, a dark shadow came out of her soul, leaving her blacked out for a few moments. Then her body faded away.

Rumours began to spread and tales were told. Years later, a class went on a field trip to the woods. Laughing, telling stories and chatting, they saw a shadow, was it her? Their faces turned pale as the shadow grew...

That class sadly disappeared forever.

Katie Harrison (10)

St Benedict's Catholic Primary School, Hindley

Miss Aspey's 'Amazing' Idea!

Miss Aspey had an 'amazing' idea, to go to a dark, creepy wood. So we all agreed and went to the campsite. We had 32 tents, but Miss Ainscough forgot to secure them, so they blew away. So we went to a cabin (again Miss Aspey's idea) and went inside to sleep.

Cameron woke up in the middle of the night, when he looked outside he saw a tall, thin entity. So he woke up Miss Ainscough, but she did not see anything. So Miss Aspey and Frankie cautiously but confidently approached the door and opened it. What happened next?

Caitlin Cunniffe (10)

St Benedict's Catholic Primary School, Hindley

Walking In A Winter Wonderland

There was once a nice girl and her friends, they were on a walk through the woods. They came across a mischievous door, it was sat in the middle of a tree, they decided to go in. There was a winter wonderland, it was beautiful, full of sweets, cotton candy on roofs and gingerbread men. They were intrigued, they spent four hours there then decided to go home. But they couldn't leave - as soon as they touched the door it vanished! They called their mums, they were worried, they didn't know what to do. What will they do next?

Laurel Carey (11)

St Benedict's Catholic Primary School, Hindley

The Screech

One day, some girls were having a sleepover. They were having a disco when they heard a loud screech coming from the back of the house. They looked but nobody was there. They ran as fast as they could, but *boom!* There he was! He ran towards the girls and they fell into a hole. It was a mirror of their world! The man was a skinny 12-foot creature, all he did was scream. The creature kidnapped the girls and they were trying to run and hide, but the creature caught them. He screamed and screeched until they eventually faded.

Mia Greeley (11)
St Benedict's Catholic Primary School, Hindley

The Haunted Prison

Four boys went into a spooky prison in the woods. It was the most haunted place on Earth and they didn't know what events were about to happen to them...

One of the boys looked behind them and saw a man sitting on the bottom of a green tree. When they got in the prison they had a look around until night-time, then it didn't take long for something to happen to one of them...

Henry heard a noise and ventured to see what it was. Then *boom!* he was gone! Because of this the others left and never returned.

Lewis Bainbridge (10)

St Benedict's Catholic Primary School, Hindley

The Camping Trip

The Year 7 class went on their annual camping trip. Once they arrived, the teachers couldn't help but notice that something was different about the forest. It wasn't a big deal as things do change. The morning after it was Year 7's first full day at the campsite. They were so excited when the teachers told them their first task was to collect logs from the forest. Off they went. They began to make their way back. There was no way back. The forest suddenly had metal fences around it. How would they ever get back?

Francesca Simpson (10)
St Benedict's Catholic Primary School, Hindley

The Mystery In The Woods

A family of three, a man, his wife and their daughter, visited their grandma who lived in a part of the woods in some flats. They arrived and settled until their daughter wondered where the grandma's carer was. So she went upstairs, to find the carer slaughtered in a pool of blood. She shouted her parents to come up (not Grandma though as she couldn't go upstairs because she was in a wheelchair). They all ran downstairs to call the police and saw the grandma's wheelchair on its side and no Grandma to be seen...

Bobby Gibson (10)

St Benedict's Catholic Primary School, Hindley

The Treehouse

Four kids went to the forest so they could sleep in a treehouse but they didn't have Internet or a signal. So if something bad happened they couldn't call for help. As they woke up, they went outside and saw a man sat next to a tree. They stared at him and he made a demonic screech so they ran! But no matter what he was always in front of them. They finally made it home safely.
The next day it was on the news.
Two years later he was captured, but one night at 11:11 they heard a demonic screech...

Thomas Metcalfe (11)
St Benedict's Catholic Primary School, Hindley

Conkers!

It is a winter's day and Reddy the red panda and Bump the aardvark go for a walk with Zack. Reddy climbs a tree and Bump goes digging. The tree Reddy climbs shakes and something hits Zack's head. A conker falls to the ground. Soon the wood's floor is filled with conkers that have fallen from the trees. Bump finds a few squashed conkers in the mud. Bump and Reddy are cold so Zack puts hats and scarves on them, then snow begins to fall from the sky. Snow fills the woods and people are happy.

Zack Prescott (9)
St Benedict's Catholic Primary School, Hindley

Five Days To Escape

Some friends went to an abandoned house and got trapped with an unworldly being. They had five days to escape. On the first day, they got the back door open but couldn't climb over the fence. On the second day, they opened the attic and got the pliers, then on the third day they got the code for the front door. On the fourth day, they almost died but they got a hammer to rip the planks of wood off the door. Now all they had to do was kill the being, which they did, and escaped the house forever.

Noah Coyle (11)

St Benedict's Catholic Primary School, Hindley

Forever Nightmare

I'm writing to tell you about a trip that went wrong. Me and my friends were telling stories, I told one about a clown. It was like I went to a different world, but when I came back my friends were gone and there was a clone above me! I ran for my life and now I'm in this cabin, if you find my letter ask the police for help, please, I'm begging you. This will be my forever nightmare that I'll live with forever. I don't know where my friends are or if they're okay.
Jess.

Ava Walsh (10)
St Benedict's Catholic Primary School, Hindley

The Anderson Centre

A few weeks ago, my class and I went to the Anderson Centre on a coach and when we got there we sensed a strange presence, but we just ignored it and got unpacked. It was late so we went to bed.

The following day we got dressed, we did some activities. Then suddenly, all of us felt the same presence we felt when we had first arrived. Next minute a rift appeared and cartoon versions of us appeared. They weren't evil. One hour later they went back to where they came from and then so did we.

Harry Addis (10)
St Benedict's Catholic Primary School, Hindley

Three Girls In The Woods

There were three girls in the woods, they were on a camping trip. They were doing activities so they hired a hut. They went on a walk in the woods and noticed someone was following them, so they started to run as fast as they could. They ran back to the hut. It went dark outside, making it harder for them to see. There was a tall man that had no face and he turned up at the hut. The girls, Mia, Emily and Katie, fled across the woods until they got to a safe place outside the wandering woods.

Emily Davidson (10)
St Benedict's Catholic Primary School, Hindley

A Different World

Once there was a boy named Oscar. He was walking in the woods, while he was walking he stepped on a hatch and fell into a different world. Oscar saw a crystal, he picked it up and a portal appeared. He went through and saw his house, he went inside and saw his mum was a zombie! So he ran out without looking back. Then a dragon came, he thought he was lost but then he found the crystal and poked the dragon in the stomach. Then the portal appeared and he got back home.

Elliot Pilkington (9)
St Benedict's Catholic Primary School, Hindley

The Missing Boys

One cold night, there were two boys on a camping trip and they saw something moving at midnight. The boys went out and they saw a creepy old man with a sleeping dart and spiky shoes and they got thrown into a white van. The old man got fed up with them and kicked them into a poison-dart frog trap! Luckily they escaped, but then a creepy clown appeared with a red balloon. One boy screamed, but then they awoke, rubbing their eyes in front of their campfire!

Harry Kay (11)
St Benedict's Catholic Primary School, Hindley

The Siren Scream

There once were two boys who lived in the middle of a forest. They wanted to get acorns for their mum, so they went further into the forest and picked up an acorn, then they heard a stomping noise. Then they saw a foot, they looked up and saw a monster! The boys dropped the acorn and ran to their house. After they got there, every night they would hear siren noises.

One night, the boys woke up at midnight and walked into the forest. There it was...

Karin Olejnikova (10)

St Benedict's Catholic Primary School, Hindley

The Bunker In The Woods

It was a sunny, warm day and we were going on a field trip to the woods. We discovered a Nazi bunker. We went in and explored what was in there, but we got lost. We tried to find a route out but it was like a maze. We saw Nazi flags and we saw bedrooms. There were weapons and ammo scattered across the floor. We had to find the way out! In the end, we had to climb to the very top and throw a crash pad down so we didn't die.

Robbie McLaughlin (10)
St Benedict's Catholic Primary School, Hindley

A Hole In The Ground

One day, as I walked home from my favourite gymnastics class, I decided to take a shortcut through the woods. All of a sudden, there was a huge hole. There was something strange about the hole. I could feel myself being dragged and I fell down, down, down. As I opened my eyes, there was magic everywhere. Fairies fluttered, unicorns danced and sparkles glistened everywhere. Just then, I was called to join the most wonderful thing ever - fairy gymnastics! My favourite thing was balancing on the beam. Just then, I blinked to find myself back in the woods again.

Martell Williamson (8)
St Margaret's CE Primary School, Stoke Golding

Bad Day, Now Great!

One day, I was taking a walk. It was a cold and miserable day. I heard something rustle nearby. Suddenly, a fox and a wolf cornered me. Strangely, they were kind and made the sun come out. They showed me lots of waterfalls. I followed them into one, into a city. There were panda policemen, firemen frogs and dinosaur doctors! But what was this? Unicorns versus centaurs playing football! I watched in interest. They kicked the ball with their back feet. I joined in, it looked fun. I got the ball... we won. I became mayor. Bad day, now great!

Charlie Crowfoot (7)
St Margaret's CE Primary School, Stoke Golding

The Magic Tree

One gloomy night, I took a stroll through the woods. It was dark and scary and creepy all around, until suddenly - ouch! I hit a tree branch. "Stupid tree!" I yelled. But then standing in front of me was the most amazing thing I'd ever seen. It was a magic portal! I decided to find out what was going on, so I entered the portal and before my eyes I saw dragons, unicorns and fairies everywhere! I saw flying tigers and mermaids in the sea.

Well, it was a really amazing day, but now it was time to go home.

Harry Macqueen (7)
St Margaret's CE Primary School, Stoke Golding

As I Wandered Through The Woods

As I wandered through the woods, one cold, dark night, I came across a mystical fog and a wolf appeared. He said, "My name is Billy, what's yours?"

"My name is Jake."

"Do you want to come and meet my friends?"

"Yes."

So I followed him and I met a spider called Aragog, an ape called Swing and a troll called Spots. But they were trying to put out a fire! So I helped by calling a water dragon and it put out the fire. After a long day, we all settled to sleep.

Archie Collis (7)
St Margaret's CE Primary School, Stoke Golding

Through The Magnificent Gates

One evening, I was taking a stroll in the woods, not really looking where I was going. Suddenly, I tripped over a huge tree root and fell on my face, when I looked up I saw some magnificent gates. I was sure they weren't there before! I walked through the gates and everything changed to the brightest colours and brightest sounds that filled the air. But the best bit was seeing the fairies fluttering all the colours of the rainbow. I had the most magical tea party which I decided to keep my secret. Then I went home.

Harriet Marshall-Rowe (7)
St Margaret's CE Primary School, Stoke Golding

The Magic Egg

As I walked through the woods, I saw something shining in the distance. I decided to investigate. I could only see a glint of sparkle, but as I got closer I realised it was much bigger, but it was covered in moss. I cleared the leaves and moss to reveal the most marvellous egg! It was blue and shiny, I was sure it was magic. Just then, it started wobbling. Glitter sparkled everywhere. With a creak and a crack, out hatched a baby dinosaur! I decided to keep him as he was so sweet. I hoped he didn't grow ginormous!

Ellie Read (7)
St Margaret's CE Primary School, Stoke Golding

A Million Years Ago

As I wandered through the woods, I tripped and found myself falling down, down, down... and I landed millions of years ago. I was a bit confused, but this changed to fear when I saw a dragon standing in front of me! However, the dragon wasn't interested in me as a huge dinosaur with big teeth was about to attack. There was an almighty battle with teeth and scales flying everywhere. All of a sudden, a tail whipped me off my feet and into the air. As I landed the air felt warmer... I was back where I started!

Sophia Hurley (7)
St Margaret's CE Primary School, Stoke Golding

Football In The Woods

One morning, as I wandered through the woods, I heard chanting in the distance. I decided to investigate. As I got closer, I couldn't believe my eyes or ears. There was a football match being played in the forest! But it wasn't any ordinary match, it was a match full of cheering crowds, which sounded quite ordinary, but the players and crowd were all animals! Today's match was rabbits versus squirrels. It was fast and furious, but the rabbits were amazing with a score of 8-0. Go rabbits!

Bobby Mawson-Eccles (7)
St Margaret's CE Primary School, Stoke Golding

The Dragon's Land

As I was walking through the woods, I thought to myself how wonderful everywhere looked. It was magical as the summer sun gleamed through the trees. All of a sudden, I saw a door. It was a bit strange to find a door in the woods. I went through the door to find myself in a magical land with fairies, unicorns and mermaids. Just then I saw a dragon, but he was crying. He had his tail trapped under a rock. I heaved off the rock and the dragon was free. "Thank you!" he called out with a smile.

Daniel Lees (7)
St Margaret's CE Primary School, Stoke Golding

A Magical Illusion

One day, a miserable boy went for a walk in the woods. The boy saw a big beam of light in the distance. The glint was from a unicorn's horn. The shimmer was so bright he squinted. The glow stopped and the unicorn turned into a troll. The boy ran, he called for help but nobody came. He just had to keep running. He ran so fast he didn't notice a huge waterfall. He fell and thought it was the end, but instead landed with a bump back in the forest. The miserable boy was now quite happy.

Lily M (7)
St Margaret's CE Primary School, Stoke Golding

The Crystal Dragon

As I was walking through the woods, I heard an almighty crash! I went to investigate. I was shocked to see a dragon who was now covered in mud and crying as she'd hurt her wing. The dragon was also crying as she was worried about her egg and asked me to look after it while she got better. I had to put the egg in my backpack and climb to the top of Crystal Mountain where the flight of dragons lived. I climbed and climbed for days until I reached the top. It was amazing. The egg was safe.

Grayson Willis (8)
St Margaret's CE Primary School, Stoke Golding

The Magical Crystal

In the woods, on a gloomy day, I wandered. I walked and walked until the air started to warm up, it was like a fire. Suddenly, a crystal fell from a tree. It was shining and glittering on the floor. As I went to pick up the crystal someone was standing in front of me. I was a bit shocked as there standing was a dragon covered head to toe in crystals. I gave the dragon back his lost crystal. He smiled and offered me a flight. We soared high above the treetops before he dropped me home.

Roy Gosling (7)
St Margaret's CE Primary School, Stoke Golding

The Magic Circle

On a spring day, as I wandered into the woods, I saw an old gnarly oak tree. It looked normal until I spotted a magic circle. I didn't know if I should... but I did! I was glad I stepped through because inside the magic circle was dragons, unicorns, princesses and fairies! It was so cool! They even let me ride on a unicorn! But then I looked at the time, it was dinner time, we were having pizza! I said goodbye and walked out the magical land.
The pizza was yum yum in my tum!

Imogen Fryer (7)
St Margaret's CE Primary School, Stoke Golding

The Whoosh!

One sunny day, I wandered into the woods. I realised that I'd lost my way, it made me worried, but even more so when I saw a flash of light. I was shocked to see a dragon. It was huge, scaly and as red as fire. I was so excited to see a dragon that I smiled. This confused the dragon who then smiled back. The dragon knelt and asked me to climb on his back. All of a sudden, we whooshed into the air and flew to a magic kingdom full of fairies. mermaids, unicorns and more dragons!

Marli Coleman (8)
St Margaret's CE Primary School, Stoke Golding

Magic Vs Monsters

As I wandered in the woods I found a unicorn, mermaid and fairy. All of a sudden, after I started playing with them, they turned into monsters! The monsters grabbed me and took me to a crystal cave. They moved a boulder to trap me. After a few weeks, I discovered a magical door. I said to the monsters there was lots of food. The monsters went to investigate and I pushed them in. I found some tools and smashed the boulder and ran home. The monsters were never seen again.

Isobella Robinson (8)
St Margaret's CE Primary School, Stoke Golding

The Magic Of The Circus

I was on my way back from the circus. When I wandered into the woods, I was daydreaming about all the tricks I had seen. I tripped over a large tree branch. As I cleaned the mud from my face, I noticed that something sparkly and bright was staring at me. At first I was scared but then I was amazed. A beautiful unicorn was doing lots of spectacular tricks; standing on one leg, twizzling around. I rubbed my eyes in disbelief and then he was gone! The magic of the circus!

Ashlyn Sharrod (7)
St Margaret's CE Primary School, Stoke Golding

A Perfect Day

I was walking through the woods when I heard a crack. When I turned around there was a huge egg about to hatch. The egg was beautiful and out popped a shiny, scaly dinosaur. He gave me a huge smile. All of a sudden, a huge shadow appeared behind me. I gulped as I knew the dinosaur mummy had returned. I thought the mummy dinosaur was about to eat me. Just then she smiled and asked if I was hungry. We went back to their cave and enjoyed a lovely party. A perfect day!

Layla Mbah (8)
St Margaret's CE Primary School, Stoke Golding

A Dragon Tea Party

One dark, cold, gloomy day, it was as quiet as a mouse. Then suddenly, I heard something. The air around me started to get warmer, I spotted what looked like a bush, but when I got closer I found out it was not a bush, it was a fire-breathing dragon! Then I realised it didn't want to be scary, it wanted to be friends. After a while I asked it if it wanted a dragon tea party and it nodded, so we had a dragon tea party where I enjoyed roasty toasty marshmallows!

Zachariah Smith (8)
St Margaret's CE Primary School, Stoke Golding

The Dragon Rocks!

As I wandered through the woods I found a magic door, I entered the door and found a dragon blowing on a rock with fire, the rock cracked open and inside were gold, gems, crystals and diamonds. There was a dinosaur coming towards the dragon and I saw them in a battle, so I snuck past but they saw me. They stopped and the dragon flew towards me and the dinosaur ran after me. The dinosaur and the dragon cornered me but then someone came to help me and saved my life!

Alfie Barlow (8)
St Margaret's CE Primary School, Stoke Golding

Magical Gaming

There was a blue crystal, I touched it and I went to the Land of Gaming! I couldn't believe it, it was magical. It was very confusing, then I realised I had to play. There were all sorts of characters, including flying pigs who were flying above my head! All the characters from my games were moving their hands and giving me high fives! Suddenly, a wizard came and was shocked I was there. He waved his magic wand and I magically found myself back in the woods.

Corey Thorp-Wrigglesworth (7)
St Margaret's CE Primary School, Stoke Golding

The Unicorn And The Dragon

One bright and sunny day, I walked through the woods. All of a sudden, I stepped into a circle of stones. It was a magic circle. I fell down, down into a magical world. There in front of me, I saw a unicorn munching. I reached out to stroke him but he changed into a dragon! I was scared. The dragon then cried a huge tear. "I just want to be friends," he cried. I pulled out some marshmallows from my pocket which the dragon toasted with a smile.

Eve Tinsley (8)

St Margaret's CE Primary School, Stoke Golding

A Fairy Picnic

As I wandered into the woods, I slipped into a dark and foggy hole. I didn't know where I was until I saw a door. I wanted to touch it but I was scared because I thought it was a trap. Then I sneezed and a fairy, who was so pretty, popped out of nowhere. I was shocked but then my tummy rumbled. I was hungry and luckily so was the fairy. We both had some berries from a bush. Then I went to a magic river and its waves took me back home.

Emily Atakli (8)
St Margaret's CE Primary School, Stoke Golding

The Magic Duck

One day, I wandered through the woods when I noticed a strange pond. It wasn't strange because I could see the fish, frogs and ducks; it was strange as the duck said, "Hello!" in a very loud and cheeky voice! I was a bit shocked. All of a sudden, the duck who had spoken began to grow! I was a little scared. It grew so big and as if by magic it turned into a dragon! The dragon then flew away and I went home.

Tobias Wakeling (8)
St Margaret's CE Primary School, Stoke Golding

Enchanted Friends

I was walking in the woods when I found an old oak tree. The tree was gnarled. Suddenly, I saw a circle that led to a very enchanted world. I saw unicorns versus flying pigs. They were having a football match. Then I saw a unicorn who was there for a second and then I saw a dragon who was hiding behind a big rock. The fairies were sparkling and chattered with their friends, they let me have marshmallows.

Lily Collis (7)
St Margaret's CE Primary School, Stoke Golding

Just In Time

It was a really bad day. I had slept in then fallen out of the door. As I was late for school I decided to take a shortcut through the woods. To make my day even worse I got chased by a pack of wolves! My heart was pounding and I was terrified! Eventually, I found a cave and they ran straight by. Suddenly, I gulped... A dragon! But it was okay, the dragon just smiled and offered to take me to school!

Bensan Elijah Karra (7)
St Margaret's CE Primary School, Stoke Golding

The Amazing Wish

As I was walking in the woods, I noticed something hiding in the bushes. It was big and furry and only when it turned around did I see huge teeth! It was a bear! There was nowhere to run and I was so scared. I just closed my eyes and made the biggest wish ever. As I opened my eyes, expecting to be eaten by the bear, I saw the most beautiful unicorn. Wishes do come true... thank goodness!

Erin Iliffe (7)
St Margaret's CE Primary School, Stoke Golding

A Perfect World

One day, I was walking through the woods, when the world ran out of ground, trees, hedges, everything! I couldn't believe it! It was like a real-life game of Minecraft! I was an expert builder so I knew just what to do. I added some grass and hedges, then built the world using all of my tools. The world was now perfect, just the way I like it!

Charlie Brocklehurst (7)

St Margaret's CE Primary School, Stoke Golding

YOUNG WRITERS INFORMATION

We hope you have enjoyed reading this book – and that you will continue to in the coming years.

If you're a young writer who enjoys reading and creative writing, or the parent of an enthusiastic poet or story writer, do visit our website **www.youngwriters.co.uk**. Here you will find free competitions, workshops and games, as well as recommended reads, a poetry glossary and our blog. There's lots to keep budding writers motivated to write!

If you would like to order further copies of this book, or any of our other titles, then please give us a call or order via your online account.

Young Writers
Remus House
Coltsfoot Drive
Peterborough
PE2 9BF
(01733) 890066
info@youngwriters.co.uk

Join in the conversation!
Tips, news, giveaways and much more!

 YoungWritersUK   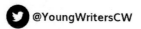 @YoungWritersCW    @YoungWritersCW